The FAB Four

ORCHARD BOOKS
96 Leonard Street, London EC2A 4XD
Orchard Books Australia
32/45-51 Huntley Street, Alexandria, NSW 2015
ISBN 1 84121 480 9
First published in Great Britain in 1997
First paperback publication in 1998
This edition published in 2003
Text and illustrations © Ros Asquith 1997
A CIP catalogue record for this book is available from the British Library.
1 3 5 7 9 10 8 6 4 2 (paperback)
Printed in Great Britain

Bad Hair Day

Ros Asquith

One

"This mirror is *not* working. But it's probably just as well. Even if I could see myself, I'd only look like the Crazed Loon from Planet Dandruff."

Lizzy Wigan was muttering furiously to herself as she stumbled through clouds of steam in search of a towel.

Why had she thought that covering her stupendously frizzy hair with a mixture that looked like a boiling swamp but smelled much worse would do any good anyway? And why make matters worse by bundling it all up in tin foil so she looked like a birthday present wrapped up by a three-year-old? She knew better than to believe all those TV ads that said Vita-Might would give her hair shine, gleam, gloss and loads of body. Come to think of it, why would hair need 'body'? That sounded rather revolting. Grump, grump, whinge, went Lizzy. Where was that stupid towel?

Lizzy was always thinking like this, but when it came to it, nothing seemed to stop her believing advertisements. She always had, ever since she was seven and had nagged her mother to buy her that *Pony 4 U* with real growing mane and tail. The mane had all fallen out the minute she combed it and the pony, which looked like a baby hippo, had been kindly nicknamed 'Baldy-coot' by her brother Ernie ever since.

"Aaaaaargh! Help!"

She had skidded on some soap.

A few of the things that always end up in the bath

Vital Essay on Egyptian ~~Hira Hera Hiroglift~~ Writing

Lizzy had hurtled into the mirror balanced on the basin, which splintered into a thousand fragments each of which, it seemed, pierced a sensitive part of Lizzy.

Why did she live in a house where perfectly dry things like socks and homework landed up in the bath while the floors were always treacherously flooded in soap and water? Or had she slipped on the remains of her bath-time banana?

Treasured Photo of → ancestor (only copy)

The bathroom floor, only recently scrubbed by Lizzy's long-suffering mother, seemed to be a river of blood. Lizzy let out a longer, higher-pitched scream.

The stupid magazine had told her:

a) That this tin foil and goo would transform her nut from a festering frizz of encrusted vipers into tumultuous tresses glistening with gloss.

b) That Tuesday would be a good day for Scorpios to fix their hair (especially if their moons were in Saturn and their names had a vowel in them).

c) That breaking a mirror was seven years' bad luck.

Or was it her Granny that said that? Anyway, she had made a vow not to be superstitious.

"Help! Mum! I'm dead!"

"You look reasonably alive," her mother said wearily, poking her face through the steam.

She seemed more concerned about the blood on her nice clean floor, Lizzy thought, than the blood on her nice clean daughter.

"Have you any idea what that mirror cost?"

"I'm bleeding to death here and all you can think about is the mirror!" yelled Lizzy.

"Nonsense!" Her mother glared at her daughter witheringly. She thought: she looks like a Crazed Loon from Planet Dandruff. But what she said was: "You have three small cuts, no more than grazes."

"But look at the blood! The place is awash! It's a battlefield."

"Could that, do you think, just possibly be caused by this?" asked Lizzy's mother, stooping to pick up an oozing tube of scarlet foam. It was Lizzy's brother's King Kong Bubble Bath.

"Ah ha," said Lizzy. So that had been the skiddy thing that had caused her horrible accident.

"Uh-huh," said Lizzy's mother.

Was it disappointment or relief that flooded Lizzy at that moment? She was ashamed to admit it was the first. However ghastly it may be to be shredded from head to foot by an exploding mirror, there were compensations: dramatic rushes to hospital, sympathy, days off school, that sort of thing.

But to find herself with only minor grazes in front of a furious parent was another can of beans altogether.

"That'll be at least ten weeks' pocket money to pay for the mirror, and at least ten minutes clearing up. Minimum."

"But Mum! It's not my fault! It's not fair!"

"Whose fault was it then? The mirror's? The bath's? Or did the basin jump up and sock you?"

Lizzy gave in. But how would she afford hair-smoothing potions now? How could she escape the embarrassing nickname of Frizzy Lizzy?

What made her even more furious was knowing that her mother worked at a chemist and could, if she wanted, get cut-price hair products. But she always chose to get other stuff instead. Stuff she was very secretive about and hid in her cupboard...

As Lizzy scrubbed away, fuming at the unfairness of Life and the Universe, her gloom deepened. The dark crimson stains of the King Kong Bubble Bath just didn't go away. How come, she thought, that when you tried to dye a t-shirt it all ran out in the first wash and turned all your underwear mauve. But when you tried to clean up perfectly inoffensive looking bubble bath that was supposed to be infant-friendly, it was like trying to sweep sand off a beach?

She thought she might have to scrub and scrub for seven years until a goblin turned up and asked her to guess his name. If she could guess it, she'd immediately get smooth hair, roller blades, castles, and stuff like that. Then her mother would have to ask *her* for money.

But with her luck, thought Lizzy, when she guessed "Rumplestiltskin," the goblin would just smirk and simper, "Tough tutus ducky, it's Derek," and vanish in a puff of smoke.

Lizzy spent half an hour scrubbing, swabbing, sweeping and picking miniscule splinters of glass from fluff-infested corners. This brought a little sympathy from her mother and Lizzy escaped to gnash her teeth next door with Claire.

Two

Comforting Claire. Smooth-haired, round-as-a-ball Claire – Eclaire to her friends. Eclaire had short, squashy, bendy legs that got tired very quickly. She had big thick heavy bunches of hair that bounced up and down and swung over her bright eyes and billiard ball nose if she ran anywhere. For these reasons, she moved slowly, which accounted, perhaps, for her curved appearance. Eclaire and Lizzy had lived next door to each other for ever. They had wept together at playgroup and howled together at nursery. They had both refused to go to Infants on their first day unless it was guaranteed that they could be together at all times.

Since those early days, Lizzy still cried at every opportunity and while she had grown lankier and frizzier, Eclaire had become smoother and rounder and calmer and sunnier by the year. They had

played houses, horses, hide-and-seek and batgirls. And just recently, they had formed the Fab Four.

They had started off as the Terrible Two, but then Flash Harriet had overheard them plotting in the playground and had asked to join. Eclaire and Lizzy thought Flash could do all the daring bits that groups were supposed to do, like catching murderers, or getting back-stage passes to concerts. And they thought maybe the Thundering

Three would be fun. Then they remembered tiny little Em, quiet as a mouse and wise as an owl, who would certainly cry if they didn't include her. They weren't sure what Em, or Owl as they called her, could do, except perhaps disguise herself as an innocent toddler to get into forbidden places, but they couldn't think of a nice way of saying 'no'. So they became the Four.

"D'you remember," giggled Eclaire, "how we asked to borrow my mum's computer to look up the 'F-Words'? She was furious!"

"Yeah. And Flash wanted us to be called the Flash Four, 'cos that's her nickname."

"And I wanted 'fat' and 'fancy'."

"And then Flash suggested 'funky' and 'freaky'."

"And then you said you wanted us to sound really tough and chose 'feckless' 'cos you thought it meant 'reckless'," giggled Eclaire.

"Yeah, and then I came up with 'phenomenal' 'cos I had that brilliant idea to look up the 'ph' words."

"You did not! It was Owl."

"Oh, yeah," Lizzy remembered that it had been Owl who'd thought of that. And it reminded her of the other reason they let Owl join. What she lacked in size, she made up for in brain-power.

However, in the end they decided on 'The Fab Four', it was less of a mouthful than the other suggestions, and it seemed to suit them perfectly!

In fact, the Fab Four hadn't actually done anything very much yet, except have secret meetings (they had had two of those), and made rather nifty membership cards on Eclaire's mother's computer.

This card certifies that
.............Lizzy..Wigan.....
is a member of
The Fab Four TOP SECRET

But the group had only been going a month and the girls were sure that some emergency would come up soon that would call for their special skills, which were...well, special.

Eclaire always had a good stock of chocolate bars. As they chatted, she and Lizzy shared six and then seven. But Eclaire had not yet remarked on Lizzy's hair. Lizzy was sure that despite the mirror incident, tin-foil disaster, King-Kong misery and all that, her hair did look a little smoother. Finally she asked:

"D'you like my hair?"

"Sure," said Eclaire kindly.

The potion hadn't worked, then.

"But it looks a little silkier, don't you think?" (Lizzy tried to sound as light-hearted as possible.)

"Mm."

Eclaire was honest. You could always say that for her. Never missed a chance to tell the truth.

"Anyway, who cares? It's only the stuff on top of your head. It's what's inside that matters."

Eclaire's hair was as smooth and shiny as a conker. How could she understand?

"But this stuff cost me three weeks' pocket money and now Mum's stopped ten weeks' more and I won't be able to do a thing."

They began cursing mothers, magazines, smoothing-goo and tin foil.

"Why is everyone trying to make us different?" said Eclaire. And promptly burst into tears.

Lizzy was shocked. Was this sunny, laid-back Eclaire? What on earth was wrong? She offered a tatty old tissue.

"I've been betrayed," Eclaire sobbed. "By my own mother. You won't believe what she's thinking of doing."

What could it be? Lizzy was intrigued.

"She's...she's...she's talking about enrolling me in Twigs and Jumbos!"

Lizzy was shocked.

Twigs and Jumbos was a slimming and exercise club for mothers and daughters. It was where barmy mothers forced their poor children to starve so that they could get into the Anorexia Model School or something daft like that. Anyway, that was how Lizzy and Eclaire saw it.

"How could she? You're lovely the way you are!" Lizzy couldn't bear the idea of a skinny Eclaire.

"That's what mothers should say...but do you know what she said to me? She said: 'Darling, I do think you need to lose just a teensy bit of weight, just a smidgeon, don't you? So you can squeeze into that pretty dress for Mary's wedding? Well, there's this really fun club we can both go to. Phyllis is going with Amelia. So you'll have a friend..."' Eclaire's voice trailed off in disgust. "Lizzy, be honest. Do you think I'm gross?"

"No, no no no. You're YOU.

You're YOU.

You're YOU,

That's WHO.

And no one else in the world will DO." shouted Lizzy.

The girls laughed. They had had a teacher when they were both in Infants who had chanted this little rhyme to them. And though they had sometimes made fun of her, they had always remembered it. Lizzy even hummed it to herself sometimes, when she was having a particularly bad hair day. At times like this, she knew frizzy hair wasn't the worst thing in the world. And neither was being plump. In fact, she'd like to be a bit plumper herself, instead of like a garden hose.

"You'll just have to say no. Anyway, your mum's thinner than a pencil. Why does she want to go?"

"To encourage me, I suppose. It's because she's

like a pencil that she wants me to be like a stick insect. She can't see that I'm naturally, well...fat."

"You're not fat. A teensy bit round, maybe."

"But my *entire* family are like telegraph poles. Why did I turn out so stumpy?"

"But you're a happy stump!"

"I was...until..."

But Eclaire was interrupted by the entrance of her mother. Mrs Pinn did indeed look like a pencil. It wasn't just that she was thin; she also had lead-coloured hair, which was swept up into a fine point at the top of her long pale face, and looked as though it needed no more than an occasional meeting with a sharpener to keep it trim.

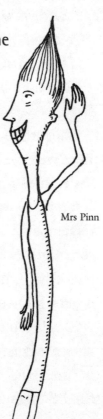

Mrs Pinn

"Claire...phone."

"Who is it?"

"Don't know, couldn't hear properly."

Eclaire rolled off to pick up the extension.

"Hi! Who is it? Who? *Who*? Of course...oh no...! Of course. Yeah. Sure. Ten minutes."

Eclaire should have known from the barely audible whisper that it must be Owl. And she was demanding an urgent meeting of the Fab Four.

"Why?" asked Lizzy, who'd been enjoying their chat and was just settling down to her half of the seventh choc bar.

"Flash's got a *big* problem."

When any one of the Fab Four were in trouble, all the others dropped everything, even choc bars. Or at least, they were supposed to. But none of them had ever been in trouble before and Lizzy was feeling lazy.

"Can't be that urgent. Couldn't it wait till tomorrow?"

"Lizzy!" Eclaire was shocked. "What did we invent the Fab Four for, if not to help each other in times of need?"

"Um..." Lizzy had thought it was more for having secrets, badges, adventures and that kind of stuff. But she realised Eclaire meant business and reluctantly heaved herself off the comfortable duvet. She loved Eclaire's room. Everything in it, including a collection of nearly a hundred cuddly toys, was soft. Big fat cushions, big fat duvet, big fat arm-chair, big fat teddies. Best of all, big fat Eclaire. Hmphhhh. She'd come round for comfort, and now she was listening to Eclaire's woes and soon she'd be listening to Flash's, too.

Three

Eclaire and Lizzy plodded down the road to Owl's house, where they found their tiny, shy friend comforting a red-eyed Flash.

Flash Harriet in tears! She never cried. Flash's life was tough, and so was she. She was sporty, quick as a flash. Flash flashed her teeth at trouble and glared at gloom. She looked flash even though all her clothes were hand-me-downs. She had red hair and small, sparkly brown eyes and a sharp nose. Her pointy ears only needed to stretch a little higher and then she would look exactly like a fox. Harriet *was* flash!

"Flash! Whatever's wrong?" asked Lizzy.

"Nothin'. I got a fly in my eye's all."

Respect. That's what Flash got.

Lizzy turned to Owl.

"OK, Owl, it's your house. You start the meeting. Then we get down to it."

Owl raised herself up to her full height (if that is the right expression for someone so tiny she could still, at a pinch, get into the under-sevens section of the Jungle Tumble) and said in her strongest voice, which was almost as loud as a gnat's whisper, so that the other three girls stopped breathing in order to catch what she was saying:

"I d-declare this meeting of the Fab Four to be an urgent and special one called at the last minute by me, Owl, to consider an emergency in the life of Flash. I c-c-command the members to inaugurate the meeting. One, two, three:

"All for one and one for all
Fatty, skinny, short and tall
Frizzy, Flash, Owl and Eclaire
Stick together, foul or fair.

Four for one and one for four
Funny, clever, rich and poor
Frizzy, Flash, Eclaire and Owl
Stick together, fair or foul."

Owl was so overcome by the effort of speech that she had to sit down and breathe deeply for ten seconds after her introduction.

Owl's room, like its owner, was minute. There was just room for a tiny platform bed with a desk and a goldfish bowl underneath it. The small walls were just high enough to hold four posters of stars. Not the outer-space kind, nor your usual film or popstars, but stars of the stage. Theatre was Owl's passion.

The three visitors were already crammed like sardines in the dark space under the bed (they plonked the unfortunate goldfish on the desk, where its bowl wobbled dangerously throughout the meeting) and Owl was forced to sit on the windowsill, where she perched, like a baby bird in its nest, swinging her little legs and gasping.

"OK," she whispered, when she had recovered her breath. "Tell them, Flash."

Flash had recovered enough to take command. After a dramatic pause, she announced: "Got a disaster. Mum's lost her job."

This was really bad news. Flash's mother was

a part-time dinner lady who earned very little, and Flash's dad had disappeared some time in the distant past. She and her mum lived with a not-very-nice and not-very-clean lodger named Snake in a flat the size of an ant's matchbox.

"Oh no!" chorused Eclaire and Lizzy. "Why?"

"Never mind why," Flash glared with the particular kind of glare that said, "I don't want to tell you," and rushed on: "It's Mum's birthday in two weeks' time. She's never had a new pair of shoes. Like *never*. I mean not ever. I'm gonna get her some. You got to help. That's it."

Flash sat down. She wasn't used to hearing her voice go all wobbly. She didn't like it. She didn't like feeling her eyes prickle like this either.

Seeing Flash upset unsettled the other three girls, too.

Eclaire felt that having a mother who could afford to enrol her in Twigs and Jumbos was not such a major problem after all. Although it showed that it was a terrible waste of money.

Lizzy cursed herself for buying hair potions and breaking the mirror and worst of all for losing ten whole weeks' pocket money which would really have come in handy just now.

Owl was feeling bad about her stash of cash that she'd saved for secret drama lessons. Not even her parents knew about this plan... they would laugh their heads off if they did. They would think there was no chance of a stuttering midget with a voice like a gnat's whisper successfully making a stage career.

She gulped and stood up.

"As ch-chair of this urgent meeting of the Fab Four, I declare that the Fab Four's mission is to raise £40 in t-two weeks for a new pair of shoes for Flash's mother. All those in favour say 'Meringue'."

And of course, everybody did.

Flash, comforted by the support of her pals, had recovered her energy and immediately launched into organising the others.

"S'easy for me. I can help up at the riding school, they like me there 'cos I know how to work." This meant that Flash knew how to muck out a stable better than her pals, because Flash had always worked hard at home to help her mother and anyway, Flash knew how to do everything better than anyone else. If someone else had been so boastful they'd have hated it, but none of the Fab Four minded Flash going on like this, because:

a)It was true and

b)The others all felt they were very spoilt compared to Flash.

"Lizzy, how 'bout cleaning cars?" said Flash.

Lizzy groaned. She was blessed with flimsy muscles and a lazy character. It was October. She would get cold. She felt six eyes gazing at her accusingly.

"Yeah, fine," she said, as brightly as possible, inwardly determined to do something else to raise her £10.

"Eclaire's easy. She can make sweets and sell 'em."

A chorus of slurps followed this suggestion. Eclaire's sweets were like something from a fairytale, with names like Nuclear Nougat and Atomic Acid Drop.

"Hmmmm. Owl..." Even Flash was at a loss.

Owl was so small and so shy, it was always difficult to think of things for her to do.

"I could w-walk the neighbour's dog," she sighed.

"Brilliant. You could practise being commanding," said Flash.

So it was settled. But a faint feeling of gloom had descended on the meeting. This was partly because nobody really wanted to work to get money for someone else but more because each of them was worried by Flash's news. They knew a new pair of shoes was not going to solve her mother's problems. Without a job, how would she pay the rent? Would Flash be thrown out of her flat? She already slept on a fold-up bed in the tiny living-room, with the unpleasant Snake in the box-room. Would she have to leave school? It made them feel insecure.

But Flash misread the mood and got upset.

"Blimey, it's not asking a lot. I'd do the same for you if your mum had a horrible skin disease all over her hands and couldn't serve dinners... I mean, if you were in trouble."

There was a silence. They all knew Flash hadn't wanted to reveal why her mum had had to give up the job. The only thing was, to pretend they hadn't heard.

Flash blustered on. "You've only got to make £10 each in two weeks. That can't be so hard, surely?"

And the other three girls knew what she meant – they were dead lucky to live in houses and have two healthy parents each.

The meeting ended grumpily, in spite of everyone's efforts to say how keen they were to help. Flash stomped off muttering that she'd clean out fifty stables a night if necessary, and some people didn't know what hard work was...

"Phew. She sounds like Mrs Graft," giggled Eclaire, but she vowed she'd invent a sherbet recipe so spectacular that she'd double the forty quid overnight.

As she and Lizzy left, they heard Owl practising commanding tones to her goldfish.

"Sit!" she murmured. "Stay... F-F-Fetch!"

The goldfish, blissfully unaware, swam on.

Four

Over the next week, Lizzy was nagged by guilt. She had to admit that she was still a whole lot more interested in trying to solve her hair problem than in stumbling about in the freezing cold with a sponge and bucket getting insulted by the neighbours.

Her first attempt at car cleaning had, it is true, been a sad experience. It was a shame she had chosen the horrible yuppie's Porsche, but she didn't think that even he would be quite so fussy over little details like smears left all over his windscreen, and a teensy scratch made by Lizzy's tank-top zip. The meanness of the very rich was something Lizzy's mum had often gone on about to Lizzy, so when Mr Yuppie swanned up saying:

"Will 50p do?" she wasn't too surprised.

But 50p for two hours' work! She'd have to clean twenty cars to make £10! Calculating at the speed of a tortoise, Lizzy reckoned that would be four cars for every school day between now and the next meeting. Or, ten cars each on Saturday and Sunday. Either way, she would be bound to miss most of the best TV. Especially now that she had to do incredibly difficult homework three nights a week because some stupid parents had nagged her school to make the kids work harder.

Argh. She couldn't possibly miss *StarStruck* because they were running a competition for tickets to see her favourite pop group, The Cruds. She couldn't miss *Petwatch* because they'd promised an item on dog allergies and she'd been trying to persuade her mother (who was allergic to dogs) to buy one for over a year. She couldn't miss *Tales of the Paranormal* or *Mysteries of the Other Side*, 'cos she'd feel a twit in the playground if she didn't know the ending of the first or the beginning of the second...the list went on. To her horror, she realised this was also the first week of a six-part series on hair. Just her luck.

To cheer herself up, now that any chance of buying hair potions had vanished for the foreseeable future, Lizzy decided to invent one.

She had, after all, spent most of the last two years reading the ingredients off the backs of bottles, and she had a fair idea of what went into most of them. True, she would not be able to find Latvian root vegetables, or Himalayan camel dung, or Essence of Queen Bee – but a lot of the stuff was available in her own home, Lizzy was certain, in her mother's cupboard...

Raiding the cupboard was fun, but produced less than Lizzy had hoped. She found:

Four cartons of Multi-vite for Fifty-somethings.

Six tubes of Hope Springs Eternal face cream.

It might make your mum's hair look like this – but not her FACE.

Ten packs of Grey-Away hair colour...

(Lizzy was very disturbed by this. She had never realised her mum dyed her hair, but she could see the Hazel Naturelle was obviously the colour her mum used).

A little tube of Opti-Myst (originally priced at a staggering £24.99) for 'minimising signs of ageing eyelids'.

← Not for pessimists

An almost empty tub of ointment for burns and scalds.

Four tubes of Shadeaway adorned with the slogan: 'Keep your bags in your hands, not under your eyes'.

A heart-breakingly vast assortment of anti-wrinkle creams with names like Fountain of Youth, Sleeko or the rather off-putting Flat-Face.

A small battery-driven thing that said it could get rid of double chins. She obviously hasn't used that, then, thought Lizzy cruelly, but she was upset to see how much her mother minded getting old. She felt even worse when she saw a bottle of pills for dog allergies. (Her mum was trying, then.) But the worst thing of all came last – a leaflet on plastic surgery.

Plastic Surgery

From this → to This!

For only 50 zillion pounds!

38

Lizzy wished she'd never looked in the cupboard, and felt sorry for her poor old mother, and she hated the thought that she might be considering a facelift. Nevertheless, she took just a couple of the Hope Springs Eternal tubes and a few dabs of the other anti-wrinkle creams – if they worked on smoothing faces they just might work on smoothing hair – and the nearly empty burn ointment tub, which was nice and big and would be good for mixing.

There was nothing else for it, she would definitely have to raid her father's 'study' (a cupboard-sized room at the top of the house) as well. She had to wait two days, during which she felt more and more guilty about the cars (she had cleaned just one more) until her father went on a trip and her mother was out.

Lizzy crept into her father's study nervously. Ever since she had been a toddler, this was forbidden ground – a mass of tottering paper and festering old tools. But his little medicine cupboard (where she once rushed many years ago to get a plaster) proved to be a treasure trove. Her father's stock of vitamins and minerals was vast. Lizzy realised that taking her father's supplies veered dangerously on the wrong side of honesty, but she would only borrow a few things, just teensy amounts...

She got:

Six capsules of Forty-Vite.

Two capsules of Agent Orange.

Numerous Mineral Powders.

Four teaspoons of Potent-Ate.

A cupful of Puma Oil.

She noticed he still had a box of children's plasters with little bunny rabbits on them. This made her want to cry.

She wanted to cry more when she found loads of leaflets on horrible things that can go wrong with you if you work too hard. Lizzy's father was always saying he worked too hard. Lizzy's mother was always saying he worked too hard as well.

"Who pays the bills? Not someone with a part-time job in a chemist's shop," he would answer.

Lizzy wished she hadn't gone into either of her parents' cupboards and that she hadn't read any of the leaflets or any of the labels on their things. She didn't like the idea of her father being so worried about his health and her mother being so worried about her looks.

Just then, the phone rang. It was Eclaire. They spoke most nights on the phone even if they had just spent the day together (which, living next door and being at the same school, they usually had).

"Just wondered how you were getting on with the scheme."

"What scheme?" asked Lizzy guiltily. (How did Eclaire know she was stealing her dad's vitamins?)

"The car cleaning of course!" said Eclaire.

"Oh great...great," Lizzy lied. "I've done a Porsche and...but how are you getting on?"

"Bit of a disaster with the first batch. But the next lot will be great. Want to come and try some in an hour?"

"N-no. Got homework," Lizzy lied again, anxious to get on with her potion.

"What? More from Mrs Prune? You poor thing! Told you you'd get extra if you drew a picture of The Cruds instead of a molar."

Lizzy reckoned the Cruds must have pretty good dentists

Lizzy winced. Mrs Prune hadn't yet seen her illustration for her Dental Health project. She'd thought she might get away with it – seeing as how The Cruds must have pretty good dentists, what with their perfect teeth, healthy vibrating tonsils and all...but she was having second and third thoughts. And now she'd lied to her best friend as well.

"Er, yeah. Well..." muttered Lizzy.

"Are you on the phone *again* Lizzy?" her mother shouted. "Have you the slightest idea what it *costs?*"

"Eclaire rang me," yelled Lizzy, "Sorry Eclaire, gotta go. Bye."

"Tell her to come round when she wants to talk. Surely it's not *too* exhausting to walk down her path and up ours? Anyway, you've only just seen her." Mrs Wigan was exasperated.

Lizzy gulped. Her mother must have come home very quietly. She might have caught her rifling through the cupboard!

After checking her mother was cosily settled with a cup of tea and the paper, Lizzy crept upstairs again. Her brother's old chemistry set was her next port of call. He had got a completely amazing one when he was nine – covered with warning labels that it was 'not a toy' and must be used with adult supervision – and he'd barely touched it. She knew exactly where it was, since Ernie was incredibly tidy. It was right at the very top of the cupboard in his bedroom.

It had been a shame, Lizzy thought later, that the chair she had balanced on to reach the very top of the cupboard in Ernie's room had had a wobbly leg. But it was certainly not her fault, just very bad luck, that as the chair had crashed to the ground it had knocked over Ernie's prized Doom Warriors collection, smashing two of his best figures. True, he had spent many hours painting and varnishing these tiny warriors, but Lizzy couldn't help hoping that he would soon realise that it had been a terrible waste of time... In fact, she hoped he might have grown out of them by the time he came back from his school trip in two days' time.

Meanwhile, she did her best with superglue, which unfortunately got encrusted in a third figure, and also dripped and hardened rather unpleasantly on the top of her brother's immaculate desk. *Why* was she the only person in the world to have a *tidy* brother? Who went scouting? And had *hobbies?* Why couldn't he run around after a ball covered in mud like everyone else's brothers?

Still, she must put such thoughts behind her and work into the night to make her Wonder Potion. Perhaps, she thought half-heartedly, it would work well enough to be sold, and raise money for Flash's mum's shoes...argh! The shoes! She would definitely clean five cars tomorrow – even if it snowed.

But Lizzy had a fantastic time making the potion. It reminded her of playing in the garden with Eclaire when she was seven. They had made a mixture of grass, mud, stale bread, washing-up liquid and gravel.

Nowadays though, Lizzy was getting really good at science. It was the only thing she ever got any praise for from any of her teachers. Most of them spent Parents' Evenings moaning about her "lack of organisational skills", or "somewhat immature attitude to study". (Well, could she help giggling when Eclaire did such excellent imitations of Mrs Graft – who did, after all, look like a duvet, despite her stern manner, thin name, razor sharp voice and all?)

But science appealed to Lizzy. Although none of her teachers could understand why it was that when it came to test tubes and formulae, scatty Lizzy became organised, daffy Lizzy became bright, clumsy Lizzy was precise and accurate. This was because Lizzy was interested, very, in science. And where her imagination was caught, the rest would surely follow.

Now, mixing her potion, she was in her element, using all her skills to develop the thing which interested her more than any other thing: the all-time super-duper Hair Potion... Lizzy's imagination ran wild as she thought of product names – Lock Lustre! Radiant Ringlets! Twinkle Tresses! But they all reminded her of silly girlie dolls' names. Maybe Diamond Dreads? Or just plain Burn-ish?

Deep into the night, Lizzy poured and mixed, whisked and warmed. Her brother's Bunsen Burner flickered under bubbling test tubes as minute amounts of minerals, vitamins and creams simmered, mingling into a glowing essence.

Lizzy began to feel gloomy as the first birds chirruped a dismal dawn chorus. Exhausted by her efforts, she remembered how none of the adults

would try her bread 'n'gravel cake mixture – just as well for them, no doubt. Her potion would probably meet the same fate.

All faith in her mixture having dwindled, Lizzy scraped it into the burn ointment tub, neatly added the name 'Burn-ish' to the label, screwed on the lid, put it by her bed and tumbled in...shocked to find that she would have to be out of bed and off to school in just ninety minutes' time. Worse still, she remembered as she fell asleep that the next meeting of the Fab Four was tomorrow, and she had only cleaned two cars!

Five

Lizzy woke what seemed like seconds later, with her mother bellowing in her ear. All the usual stuff: "Do you think this entire house revolves around you? Do you want another detention for being late? Just *look* at the state of your room! Why can't you be more like your brother? And for goodness sake drag a comb through your hair, you look like a Yeti!"

This last remark stung Lizzy. She had so wanted to try the potion immediately, but now it would have to wait in the crazed rush for school.

Remarkably, Lizzy staggered into her class milliseconds before the bell. Miraculously, she stayed almost awake for most of the day. Incredibly, in the moments she did snooze off, no teacher noticed.

Lady Luck is with me, she thought. Tonight I

will find five generous lottery winners whose squeaky-clean cars need just a whisper of a polish and they will shower me with dosh and gratitude. Tomorrow I will surge, triumphant, to the Fab Four meeting, my newly be-potioned tresses streaming down my back like...well, um, like hair, I guess...

There were moments when even Lizzy could see there was something just the teeniest bit daft about comparing that old stuff we all have on top of our heads with waterfalls, streams, curtains, weeping willows or whatever. But although she was truly concerned about getting the money for Flash's mum, she was desperate to try out her potion. Just the thought of it, tingling in its tub beside her bed, kept her going for the boring day in which not a single bit of information given by her poor teachers remained inside her addled brain.

Alas and woe. When Lizzy returned home and raced to her room and rushed to her bedside table she found – no potion!

Just a note, which read:

This room is a disgrace! Pigs would be ashamed to live in it. Bedbags would pack their bugs. TIDY UP! Or lose two weeks' pocket money.

At first, Lizzy had a violent fit of giggles when she saw her mother's mistake in writing 'bedbags' instead of 'bedbugs' and 'bugs' instead of 'bags'. Then the note, combined with the Tragedy of the Missing Potion, sank in. Exhausted as she was, Lizzy collapsed in tears. Why couldn't her mother take some anti-bad temper pills or some Calmo For Mums Who Worry Too Much, instead of wasting precious time on what her daughter's room looked like? *She* didn't have to sleep in it, after all.

Lizzy stomped downstairs waving the note:

"Why should I? Who cares about tidying rooms when there are people out in the world who haven't even *got* a room?"

"Keeping yours untidy won't help *them*, will it?"

Her mother was speaking quite kindly, as she could see Lizzy was overtired, but Lizzy fumed on.

"I don't see why clothes have to be in cupboards! Let's give the cupboard to the poor!"

"Carry it downstairs and take it to the Homeless Centre if you want," said her mother cheerfully. "But don't expect me to help."

Lizzy stormed on to herself. Clothes were for wearing, weren't they? While you were wearing them, they were doing their job of keeping you warm or trying to make you look nice, or whatever it was they were supposed to do, and when they were off you, they were useless. So what did it matter if they were on the floor, or tangled decoratively round the bed legs or tastefully overflowing from the top of her desk as Lizzy's were? And if bedbugs would pack their bags, then yippeeee! Only adults cared about this stuff. They piled all their hang-ups onto helpless children who had enough worries, what with missed homework, missing hair potions, no cars cleaned, friends' mothers with terrible illnesses and no jobs. With the Fab Four meeting looming...Lizzy howled.

She cleaned up just the same. Her reasons were as follows:

1. She could not afford to lose two weeks' more pocket money.

2. Finding all the wrinkle stuff and hair dye had made her feel sorry for her mother.

3. She thought her mother must have confiscated the potion and didn't have the courage to ask her for it now – perhaps, after cleaning her room, she would feel on stronger ground.

4. She didn't like to admit it, but her room was repulsive. Even her prized brush and comb collection (which included an unopened 1959 pack of kirby grips her mother had given her, and a Victorian dolls' house comb that was smaller than a fingernail) which Lizzy usually took pride in, was all over the place.

5. She didn't like to admit this either; but it gave her a good excuse not to go out in the freezing fog cleaning cars...

Lizzy spent the next two hours weeping into old felt-tip pens, little bits of fluff held together with glue, kleenex that had seen too many noses, ancient socks, and all those other curious oddments that gather in rooms where no cleaner ever treads. It's as if, thought Lizzy, they are all taking shelter. She imagined the paperclips, buttons, bus tickets and old lolly sticks, all marching from pockets, drawers and mysterious hidey-holes in other corners of the house, to the safety of her room: the Hoover-Free Zone. This vision overcame her so much that she was quite unable to throw anything away, but instead created an 'oddments bowl' into which she chucked everything that didn't have a natural home of its own. At least they'd all be happy there together, and maybe the bus ticket would get on with that nice little receipt from the chemist's... At this point Lizzy knew that she was, for once, what her mother accused her of being nearly every day, overtired.

But at least her room looked habitable and she had to admit it was much more cosy to think of coming up to bed in here than to the hell-hole she had created before. But it was a small comfort when she thought about tomorrow.

Lizzy had earned just £2.50 (the owner of the second car, being a nice kind poor person, had at least given her £2. But still, it was pathetic...). She had left it far too late to clean any more cars now and she certainly didn't have the courage to ask her mother about the potion. She was too scared about having 'borrowed' the ingredients.

She felt particularly worried about the return of Ernie. He would be back from his school trip tomorrow evening and his first thought would be his Doom Warriors. Anyway, her mother had probably thrown her potion out...a thought which only deepened Lizzy's despair.

Tea-time was less than happy.

"You're looking pale," said her mother.

"Ugh," grunted Lizzy.

"And you have rings under your eyes."

"Mmm," mumbled Lizzy, pushing a limp fish

finger round her plate. Her mother didn't mention the strange state of her hair, which now looked as though an extremely depressed family of bears had wandered into it to hibernate, but had found it too gloomy and left.

The tea from hell was followed by a lukewarm bath into which Lizzy desperately plunged her mane, only to find that both her shampoo and her conditioner were empty. Her wig was now so straggly that even the most expensive comb in her collection made no headway.

That night she dreamt she was in the clutches of a crazed scientist who was using the static electricity created by her hair to power a gigantic rocket.

"Inside zis rocket," bellowed the scientist, who had pea-green hair and an enormous beard full of worms and crumbs, "eeees efferybody you haff effer luffed."

"No!" shrieked Lizzy. "Not my family! Please!"

"Yusssss! All your femily. All your frendz! And weeth ze amaaaazing power of zis magic hairdo of yours, I am goink to send zem all into Outer Space, where zey will circle ze planet for eternity. Or until zey are burrrrnt to a crisp! Hah! hah! hah!"

"But why? Why? How can I save them?"

"Eeet iss too late for that! Ifff you had cleaned ze rocket and smoothed your hair, you wouldn't be in zis situation! Hah! hah! hah!"

Lizzy stared aghast into the rocket. There were her parents...Ernie...her Gran...her cousin Cedric...Auntie Violet...Flash...Owl...Eclaire! If only she had used her potion, then the scientist wouldn't be able to use her hair, then...then...

Lizzy woke in terror, realising as she did so that the rocket had been shaped like a giant shoe.

Six

Late for school, Lizzy stopped to dip a single Krisped Ricey in a drop of milk.

"I had a dreadful nightmare," she tried to explain to her mother.

"I said you shouldn't watch *The Paranormal Files*, or whatever it's called," said her mother unsympathetically. "Your auntie Vi just rang – she's bought a new car! Called an Orbiter!"

Lizzy nearly choked on her single Krisped Ricey. "An Orbiter! I'm psychic, I knew it."

As she was tearing around collecting her school things, her mother said, "By the way Lizzy, that burn cream I found in your room proved an absolute wonder! I scalded myself quite badly yesterday, and had a terrible blister...but the cream made it burst and then heal! I couldn't believe my eyes!"

But Lizzy was tearing out of the door. What was

it her mother had been saying? Who cared? She couldn't bear another telling off for being late. And now she was worrying about her Auntie Vi on top of everything else. Orbiter. Would the new car be safe? Had she been sold it by a man with a beard? The world was a cruel and menacing place, full of giant shoes and dangerous cars – all waiting to be cleaned...

As the grisly day wore on, Lizzy spent all her time avoiding Eclaire and Flash and thanking heaven that Owl was in a different school. She had never dreaded a Fab Four meeting before. Why hadn't she stayed home ill? Or run away, or something sensible like that? How would she sneak back all the ingredients she had 'borrowed'? What would her brother say about his Doom Warriors?

It wasn't until lunchtime, revived by a nibble of pasta, that Lizzy felt her self-pity lift to the extent that she thought about what her mother had said as she'd left the house.

She remembered, with horror, that she had put her hair potion in a jar marked 'Burno – for minor scalds and burns'! All she had done to the label was change the name 'Burno' to 'Burn-ish'! And...her mother must have used it! On her skin!

What had she said? Lizzy struggled to remember. Oh no! Something about a giant blister! That was it:

"By the way, Lizzy, that 'burn cream' of yours proved an absolute blunder! I scalded myself quite badly yesterday, and had a terrible blister and the cream made it worse, and then a weal... I couldn't believe the size..."

Lizzy froze. What a disaster! The cream had already made the blister worse and produced a horrible weal, and that had been at breakfast time! Something much, much worse might have happened by now! Supposing it was like that terrible Blob in *The Paranormal Files*? Lizzy had pretended that the Blob hadn't scared her at all when she was discussing it with her friends in the playground. But it had actually been a terrifying slimey violet goo that had slurped all over people. It had turned them into a mass of sores and then sucked their brains out to send to a Giant SuperBrain on another planet! *Violet* goo! Maybe that's why she dreamt of Auntie Violet! She must get hold of her mother!

To the surprise of the odd assortment of kids with whom she was eating lunch, Lizzy announced, "I'm dying."

Everyone immediately pushed their plates away and started having anxiety symptoms. They felt a bit queasy themselves...was there a lunatic in the kitchen trying to poison the dinners? See? That was what you got if your parent was too busy or too poor to provide you with a decent packed lunch of crisps and chocolate...

Lizzy staggered into the school office. The secretary, a calm and efficient woman called, very suitably, Mrs Placid, immediately summed up the situation: miserable girl pretending to be ill but probably suffering from:

a) Bad conscience
b) Broken heart
c) Family tragedy

Mrs Placid, a kind hearted soul, hoped Lizzy's obvious despair was due to cause (a) but called in Mrs Scalpel, the first aider, just to be

Mrs Placid, in a fierce mood

on the safe side, put herself on Tissue-Alert and agreed that Lizzy could phone her mother. Sometimes, although by no means always, a mother was the best person in such circumstances.

But when she got through to the chemist's shop, Lizzy heard the words she dreaded:

"Your mother's gone home, love."

Trembling, she phoned home.

No answer.

Panic!

"Why not try your father, dear," suggested Mrs Placid.

"He's away!" sobbed Lizzy, by now hysterical.

"My dear, why not tell me about it."

And Lizzy, comforted by the warm, motherly figure of Mrs Placid, poured out the whole, shaming story of hair potions and her terror that she had killed her own mother!

Mrs Placid plied her with tissues, but Mrs Scalpel who had just arrived took a different line.

"Foolish girl! Have you never heard of the terrible dangers of putting things in the wrong bottles? There was a barman once, who stored *bleach* in an old white wine bottle! Of course, one day he gave it to a customer by mistake. The consequences were *fatal*."

Lizzy wondered why Mrs Scalpel had chosen to be a Special Needs teacher with extra responsibility for First Aid.

Mrs Scalpel in a good mood

There must be lots of jobs going as a prison warder, or torturer...

At that moment, the phone on Mrs Placid's desk rang.

Lizzy froze.

She knew that there were a trillion phone calls every day to a school secretary. But she also knew that this phone call was about her mother.

She was right.

"Yes," said Mrs Placid, placidly. Then, "Oh dear," (less placidly) then, "Of course, I'll put her on. She's just here."

Turning to Lizzy she said, "It's your granny, dear."

Lizzy grabbed the phone, but all she heard were clicks and whirrs followed by silence.

Unbelievable! Her gran's money had run out!

But obviously she would ring again...

"Now don't worry," calmed Mrs Placid, pulling more tissues out of the box. "All your gran said was, well, your mum's had to go to the hospital and she wants you to go to your gran's after school in case she isn't back. Your gran will be home any minute."

"Hospital!" She had killed her own mother! She *knew* it!

Lizzy waited for her gran to phone again – surely she would reverse the charges? But she didn't, so Lizzy got permission to go over to her gran's straight away.

As Lizzy hurtled to her grandmother's house, she understood the meaning of the phrase, 'Her heart was in her mouth', for the first time. Panting, sweaty, dishevelled, her hair (who *cared* about *hair*?) standing up like a porcupine's prickles, she arrived at her grandmother's bungalow and battered at the door.

"Please be in, please, please, *please*," she moaned.

"Hold your horses, darling," her grandmother fussed and fiddled with bolts. "What's the hurry?"

"Mum, Mum, I must ring Mum!"

"Goodness, sweetheart, you do panic..." But Lizzy wouldn't listen.

"Gimme the hospital number – quick, Gran. It's a *real* emergency. I must tell the doctors looking after Mum as much as I can about the deadly cream. It's like when a toddler swallows pills. I have to get straight in there with details, otherwise...otherwise..."

Lizzy dialled, distraught, asking for Casualty and babbling about the cream. It took her a few minutes to understand what the nurse on the other end was saying. No one answering her mother's description, or using any name remotely like Mrs Wigan, had been admitted for emergency treatment at the hospital that day. No, there was no one of that name, *really*. Perhaps it was another hospital?

"She's not there," Lizzy shouted frantically to her gran. "Maybe she's dead already."

Between lurching sobs, she told her grandmother her fears.

"Goodness me, what a drama," her grandmother sighed, offering Lizzy a dainty handkerchief, frilled with lace. Lizzy didn't like to use it even in these desperate straits.

"If only you listened, darling. Your mother's gone in for a routine checkup, that's all. She wouldn't have gone to Casualty for that, would she? She just forgot to mention it this morning. She phoned me so that you wouldn't go home to an empty house. I'm sorry I phoned you while I was at the shops, and I didn't have time to explain properly. But I had no idea you'd be in such a flap. Anyway, darling, a little bit of ointment couldn't *kill* anyone, could it?"

It took a few moments for these words to sink in. A routine check up? Was that all? But even so, Lizzy was unconvinced. She phoned Flash's number and left a hurried message on her answerphone. She said that she feared her mother was desperately ill and that it was all her fault and she couldn't possibly come to the Fab Four meeting that evening as she had to wait for news. Lizzy was aware, while leaving the message, of a stab of guilt. If her mother wasn't ill, then she was using her to get out of an awkward situation. Surely she wasn't doing that really, was she? She pushed the thought away.

"I'll ring outpatients, then," she told her Gran in a calmer voice. "They should know about the cream anyway."

As Lizzy was dialling, the doorbell rang. And there were the warm smile, the rosy cheeks, the sparkling eyes, of her beloved mother...

"You're alive! You're alive! You're alive!"

Her mother looked puzzled.

"How reassuring. I only went in for a check up you know – didn't Gran tell you?"

Lizzy knew she had to explain herself. She did.

She left nothing out, not even the Doom Warriors, despite the fact that they would swallow up a month's pocket money. The tiny figures, which only cost about 2p to make, were a huge craze, and were sold at enormous prices to small boys. Lizzy also admitted to taking some of her dad's

Doom Warrior
Zang, Chieftain of the 96th Battalion
of Mega-Nerds. (Ten times actual size)

stuff (though without going into all the details) and, blushing deeply, she finally squeaked out what she had taken from her mother's cupboard.

"And all for the sake of my stupid hair..." she ended, lamely.

Mrs Wigan looked very stern. "Lizzy, do you know how dangerous it is to play around with chemicals and medicines? You must promise me never ever to do anything like this again. As well as that there's a fine line between borrowing and stealing, you know."

Lizzy nodded and looked at her feet.

"Not to mention invasion of privacy," sighed Mrs Wigan. "How would you like it if someone read your private diary?"

Lizzy felt terrible.

"Everyone knows..." her mother went on, "that it's dangerous to put things in the wrong bottles. There was once a barman who put bleach in an old white wine bottle. Of course one day he gave it to a customer with *fatal* results!"

Lizzy looked up and stared at her mother. It made her wonder if all adults went on courses to terrify children. Were they all told the same story? Or were there barmen all over the world doing this sort of thing and should she never order lemonade with true peace of mind again? Just then Lizzy heard her mother say:

"Thank you for being honest. I was going to ground you but I know you must want to go to your Fab Four meeting later...and I'll let you go as long as you promise to pay for everything you have borrowed or broken."

Naturally, Lizzy had mixed feelings at her mother's kindness. Her joy at having a live mother was swiftly watered down by the knowledge of her pathetic failure to clean cars. She had put her own appearance before the interests of her friends.

She knew that her half-formed plan to beg some money off her mother to take to the meeting was a goner. She would be in debt for the Doom Warriors for ever as it was, never mind the chemistry set, which she had a horrible feeling had cost over £20.

Maybe she could plead illness again. No. She'd been stupid enough in the last week already, she'd bite the bullet, come clean to the Fab Four, have a stiff upper lip, put her shoulder to the wheel, nose to the grindstone, soldier on...blah...blah...what was she whingeing about? Her mother was alive!

Seven

Lizzy arrived breathless at the Fab Four meeting and was moved by the excitement with which her mates greeted the news of her mother's miracle recovery. (Eclaire had told them all about the garbled answer-phone message.) But she didn't dare mention the tiny amount she'd raised, and wondered whether she *could* use her mother's illness as an excuse. She felt relieved to find that she couldn't sink that low.

Nervously, she waited for the other three to reveal their earnings, struggling with her own conflicting feelings. First, wouldn't it be great if they'd all done badly, so she wouldn't be shown up? And second, wouldn't it be great if they'd all done brilliantly so that her failure wouldn't matter (in the Great Scheme of Things) and at least Flash's mum would get her shoes. Lizzy knew which was better, but she couldn't tell what she really wanted.

To her amazement, it turned out that teeny, timid Owl had done amazingly well.

"Um, I m-m-made £19 by walking..."

"Running, you mean," laughed Flash.

Owl smiled and went on, "I took out f-four greyhounds for the local d-d-dog track."

Lizzy stared in amazement at Owl.

"I don't know why they p-paid me so m-much," whispered Owl, "but I think it was 'cos..." (her voice sunk even lower so that the others had to strain forward to hear and nearly toppled off Eclaire's bed), "...th-they felt sorry for me."

Lizzy examined her feelings. Hmmm. Not bad. She admired Owl's modesty. She admired her, um, doggedness. She smiled at her own joke. Maybe things were getting better...

It was Flash's turn.

"And I earned £11 by slaving in the stables from 6 o' clock every morning," said Flash. "But, phew, I'd have run with them greyhounds if I'd known what the rate was," she added, smiling at Owl.

So Flash had only just topped the £10 mark. Lizzy was surprised. She'd felt sure that Flash would have got to £15. She'd had no idea how little money Flash made from mucking out stables. It was exploitation, it really was. But then, she did get free rides...didn't she? Lizzy blushed, thinking that her mother had offered her riding lessons and she hadn't wanted them.

But Eclaire was blushing deeper.

"I feel terrible," she squawked. "I made a whole batch of Sherbet Grabs...and, er, I ate them."

Shocked silence. Lizzy didn't know whether to laugh or cry. She felt really sorry for Eclaire...and yet...it was so wonderful to hear that someone else had messed up, too.

Eclaire rushed on: "...and then I mixed enough stuff for sixty Toffee Tinglers and...and...I burnt the mixture. So, I just panicked and made peppermint creams and all I got was...was... £7.50. I'm so sorry, Flash, I feel a real failure not getting to £10. But I'll put £2.50 in from my money box. Promise."

To everyone's horror, Eclaire seemed on the verge of tears. Probably her mean mother nagging her about Twigs and Jumbos again, thought Lizzy grimly. She realised she had not been thinking very much about her friend over the last week. Anyway, Eclaire had raised £5 more than Lizzy had, and now the horrible moment of reckoning was near and Lizzy once again understood the meaning of having her heart in her mouth.

"Don't worry, Eclaire," said Flash heartily, making Lizzy feel worse. "You won't have to do that. We've still got to hear from Lizzy and I bet she's done brilliantly."

Thud, thud, thud. Pound, pound, pound. Tremble, tremble, blush.

"Let's see, how much've we got?" Flash did a quick calculation. "Look! Owl's done so well that all we need's £2.50!"

Deliverance! Lizzy couldn't believe her luck! £2.50 was all they needed, and £2.50 was all she had.

Sheepishly, Lizzy pulled out her money.

"I'm sorry, but I've had a terrible week. I've been really selfish and all I've had time for is my stupid hair. But you've all been so great. I think I've learned...um...some sort of lesson...maybe," she ended lamely.

"Lizzy, you *know* I love your hair," shouted Eclaire.

"Yeah. You wouldn't be *you* without it," agreed Flash.

"B-but I won't c-call you Frizzy again if y-you don't like it," murmured Owl.

"Thanks, Owl," said Lizzy, touched by these speeches, "but I can take it."

Happy to be such good friends and warmed by the thought of the gorgeous red leather shoes that Flash would be buying immediately, the four clasped hands, bellowed "Meringue!" and closed the meeting:

"All for one and one for all,
Fatty, skinny, short and tall.
Frizzy, Flash, Owl and Eclaire
Stick together, foul or fair.

Four for one and one for four,
Funny, clever, rich and poor.
Frizzy, Flash, Eclaire and Owl
Stick together, fair or foul."

Eight

Lizzy's good mood took a dive when she got home.

"You *smashed* all my Doom Warriors!" screamed Ernie.

"I smashed *two*," yelled Lizzy.

"I spent years and years painting them," groaned Ernie.

"Oh yeah?" sneered Lizzy.

"They're my *best* thing," shouted Ernie.

"Oh grow up. They're just stupid little war toys. War toys for silly boys," snapped Lizzy.

"Lizzy! I'm ashamed of you," her mother stormed in. "I think you should apologise to Ernie right now. It's the least you could do, especially after our conversation..."

At this point, Lizzy's mother gave her one of her looks. Lizzy's mother's looks could wither fruit on the vine. But Lizzy was so exhausted by the emotions of the last two days and lack of sleep, that she could not do the right thing. She locked herself in the bathroom and howled instead.

No one came.

She howled louder.

Silence.

She fled to her bedroom and found her newly tidied nest was a whirlwind of activity. Ernie was leaping up and down on her prized collection of brushes and combs.

"Ratfink! My *combs*!"

"*That's* for my Doom Warriors," (thump, wallop, clunk). "And *that's* for my chemistry set!" (pull, yank, twist).

"My *hair*! Let go let go let go!"

"And *that's* for glue on my desk!" (crash, zergunk, squelch).

"No-o-o-o-o-o! Not my kirby grips! No! They're a collector's item! They'll be worth money!"

But the kirby grips were scattered, the tiny comb no bigger than a fingernail was stamped on.

The brush shaped like a hedgehog was split...

"That's enough. *Enough*!" yelled Mrs Wigan, wondering not for the first time, whether she had raised two children or a couple of werewolves. Just as she had herded them into separate corners, the phone rang.

"If it's for me, say I'm dead," Lizzy cried despairingly.

But it was Flash's mother, ringing to tell them about the amazing shoes. Ringing to tell Lizzy's mum how wonderful her daughter was, how wonderful all the girls had been, what an adorable thing to do. And so on.

Mrs Wigan put the phone down with the ghost of a smile.

"At least you've made an effort to help someone else for a change, even if it was a small effort," she added.

It's lucky she doesn't know how small, thought Lizzy.

Her mother continued, "Actually, Lizzy there's something *else* you've done recently I want to talk to you about."

Help! thought Lizzy. What now?

"That mixture you made is proving quite interesting."

Lizzy scuffed her toes on the floorboards. There was something sinister about this. Was she going to be imprisoned now for making explosives?

"Look, I only meant it to be a hair potion, really!"

At the sight of her daughter's sad face, Mrs Wigan decided she couldn't torture her child any more and she spilled the beans.

"It seems your mixture might be good for all sorts of burns and rashes – maybe even eczema."

As her mother's words sank in, Lizzy felt very strange. Something nice was happening at last. And then something even better happened.

"I gave some to Harriet's mother. And she just told me that it seems to be working on her skin complaint."

"But how did you know about her skin thingy?"

"She came round to the chemist looking for something to get rid of the itching, and I told her I'd used some on my burn and it was very soothing. She said she might as well try it as nothing else had worked."

Lizzy was over the moon. Maybe Flash's mum would get her job back!

She'd been lousy at cleaning cars, she'd robbed her family, but she'd saved Flash's mum.

"Remember, Lizzy, you must keep your experiments to the science lab from now on. Your potion could have been really dangerous. But who knows, in the future you might invent a new cream, and that would be much more important than a beauty treatment, wouldn't it?"

Lizzy blushed deeply at the thought that all she had cared about was her hair. But she blushed for her mother, too, at the thought of all the anti-wrinkle creams...

For a moment, a wonderful, exhilarating moment, she had a dream...a vision of herself being awarded the Nobel Prize for Science... she saw a blue plaque on the side of the house that read:

DAME ELIZABETH WIGAN, SAVIOUR OF HUMANITY, LIVED HERE.

And then reality dawned.

She'd never be able to remember exactly how much of each thing she put in the potion – even if she could bring herself to admit about the wrinkle cream and the Oil of Puma. Also, she knew there had been traces of the original burn ointment in the jar – she had no idea how much.

"But I'll never be able to remember all the stuff I put in!" she wailed.

"That's not the point, sweetheart. What this shows is that you might be good as a scientist of some sort, and perhaps one day you'll invent something truly marvellous. I'm proud of you, I really am."

"I only did it for my stupid hair."

"Lizzy, I love your frizz!" said her mum.

Lizzy felt quite tearful. It had been her mother who had always nagged her to brush and comb her hair all her life. It had been her mother who had bought her slides and ribbons and combs and hairbands as a little girl and who had encouraged her to start the brush and comb collection. It had been her mother who had made the terrible mistake of marrying a man called Mr Wigan, thereby ensuring that her daughter would be teased for eternity about her wig. And now, here was her mother – alive, alive! – saying she loved her frizz! Maybe her frizz wasn't so bad after all, then. Had she been doing all this for her mother, without even being aware of it?

As if reading her mind, Mrs Wigan gave her daughter's hair a tender stroke. Then she gave her daughter a tender hug. "Really, I *do* love your frizz."

"And I love your wrinkles," said Lizzy, hugging her back.

Whooops. Why had she said that?

But Mrs Wigan surprised Lizzy with a great roar of laughter. Then Ernie came in and offered to shake Lizzy's hand and forget everything – not really, he had green slime hidden in his paw and was anxious to put as much of it as possible on Lizzy. But you can't have everything.

Lizzy went to bed that night happier than she had been for a long while. She realised the

Fab Four had another big task to do...save Eclaire from Twigs and Jumbos...but that could wait until tomorrow.

Read more about
Frizzy Lizzy, Flash,
Eclaire and Owl
in the other FAB FOUR books.

1-84121-482-5

Frock Shock!

Eclaire's happy being fat, but her pencil-thin
mum has got other ideas. Can Eclaire escape
the horrors of the Twigs and Jumbos club
and keep fat rather than fit?

1-84121-478-7

The Love Bug

Flash normally prefers mucking out to
making out, but when she meets the gorge
new stable lad, Tom, her favourite pony, Flame,
is quickly forgotten. Will Flash come to her senses
in time to save Flame from the knacker's yard?
And who's going to give Flash some top tips
on her make-up bag?

1-84121-476-0

Drama Queen

Owl's so shy she's never taken part in anything
involving more than two people – even a
conversation. But Owl's got big dreams and
nothing's going to stop her being in the school
play. Will she get the starring role or should
she play something a little quieter, a piece
of scenery perhaps?

Three's a Crowd

The Fab Four are off on a school trip.
But can Owl cope with taking part in scary
activities like abseiling, white-water canoeing
and worst of all, sharing a cabin with bully
bossy-boots, Bernice Berens? She'll have the
Fab Four to help, of course!

All for One

When Eclaire's dad gets a new job at the other
end of the country, it looks like the Fab Four are
finally going to have to split up. But the friends
won't be parted that easily. They've got a sassy
new plan to get Eclaire's family to stay...but it
could land them in a whole lot of trouble...

More Orchard Red Apples